# THE BULLY NAMED SAUL

## WRITTEN AND ILLUSTRATED BY

# ERIC C. GOOSE

## ©COPYRIGHT 2021

THE MATERIAL IN THIS BOOK MAY NOT BE SUITABLE FOR SOME PEOPLE. THERE ARE IMAGES OF SMOKING AND VIOLENCE.

# PREFACE

THANK YOU FOR READING THIS BOOK. THE BULLY NAMED SAUL WAS WRITTEN AS A POEM AND IS LOOSELY BASED ON REAL LIFE EVENTS. KINDA....

HERE'S THE TALE OF THE BULLY, SAUL.

HE STOLE' MY BIKE—TOOK MY BALL.

HE'LL CALL YOU SHORT WHEN YOU ARE TALL.
HE WILL FIGHT YOU AT THE MALL.
'TIS THE TALE OF THE BULLY NAMED SAUL.

WALKING HOME 'TWAS GETTING DARK.
I SAW BERNICE DOWN AT THE PARK,
HER EYES WERE WET FROM HER TEARS.
HER FACE WAS FROZEN FROM HER FEARS.

WHEN I ASKED HER TO EXPLAIN,
SHE CRIED SOME MORE I FELT HER PAIN.
SHE TOLD ME IT WAS A BOY
WHO KNOCKED HER DOWN AND TOOK HER TOY.

"WAS HE WIDE OR WAS HE SMALL?"

"NO!" SHE SAID, "NOT AT ALL.

HE WAS SLIM, YET BIG AND TALL."

THEN I KNEW IT MUST BE SAUL.

TO HAVE NO FRIENDS TO CALL YOUR OWN.
NO ONE TO BUY AN ICE CREAM CONE.

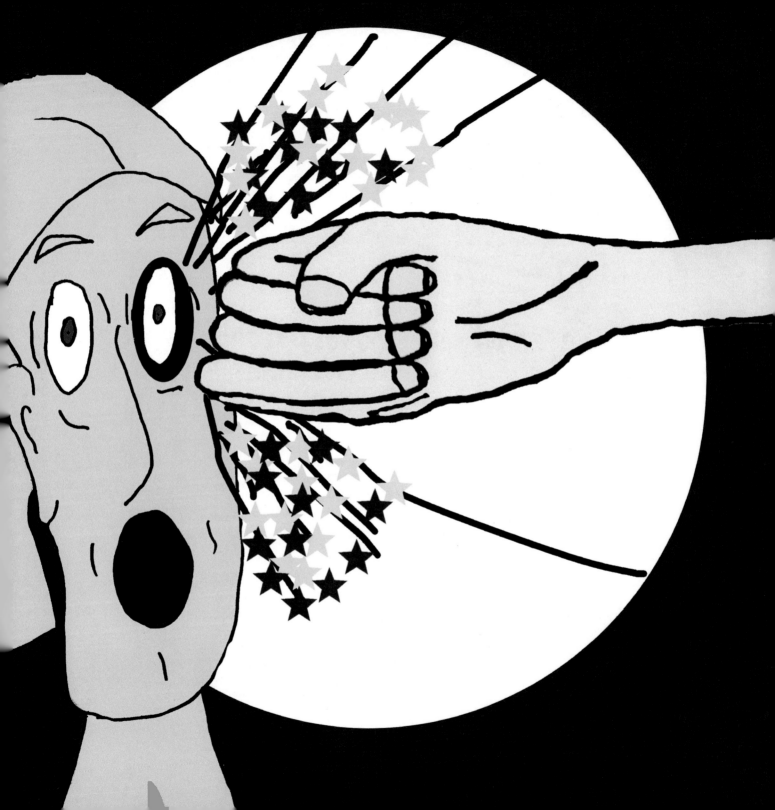

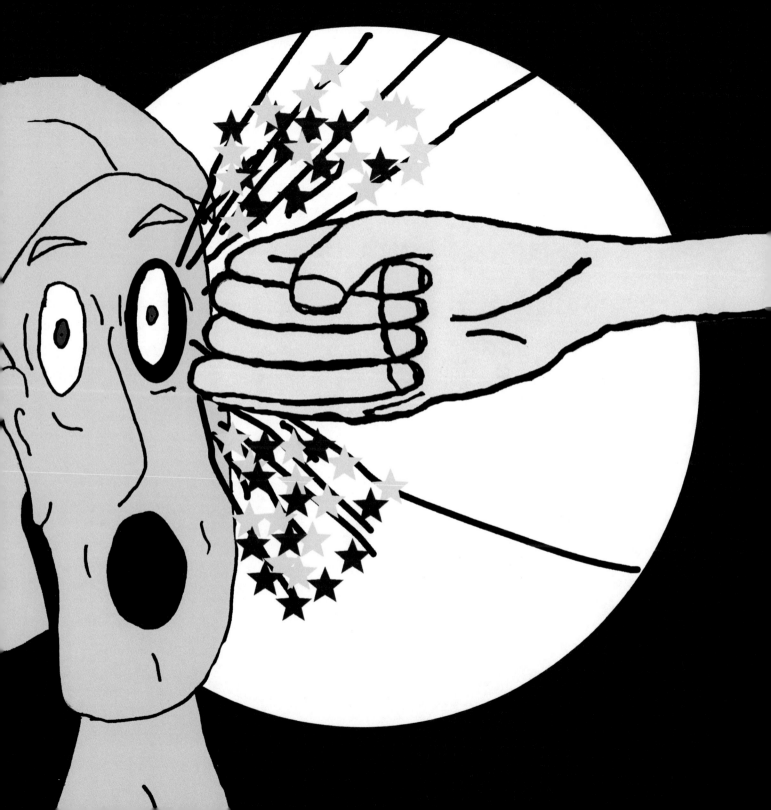

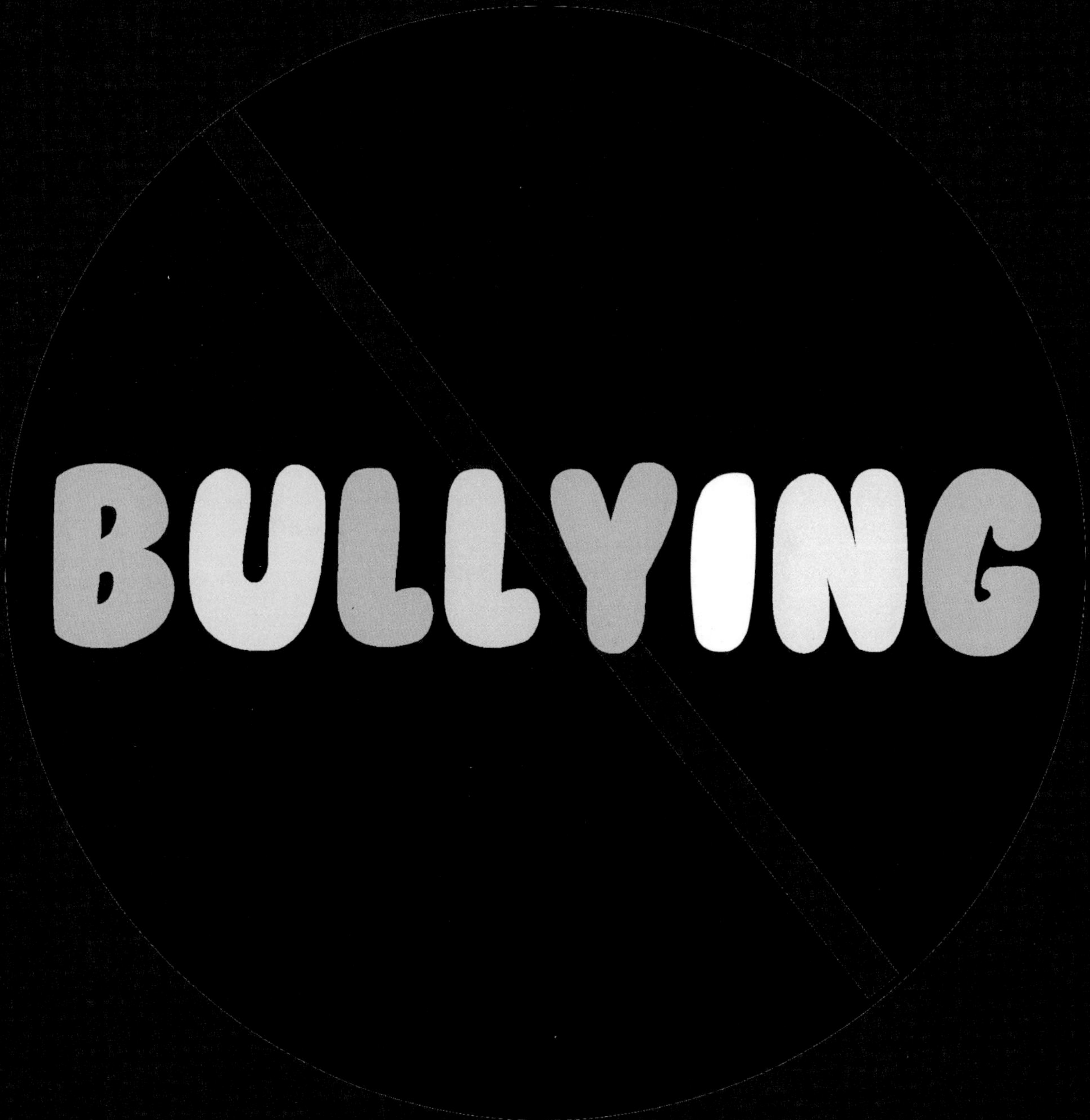
BULLYING

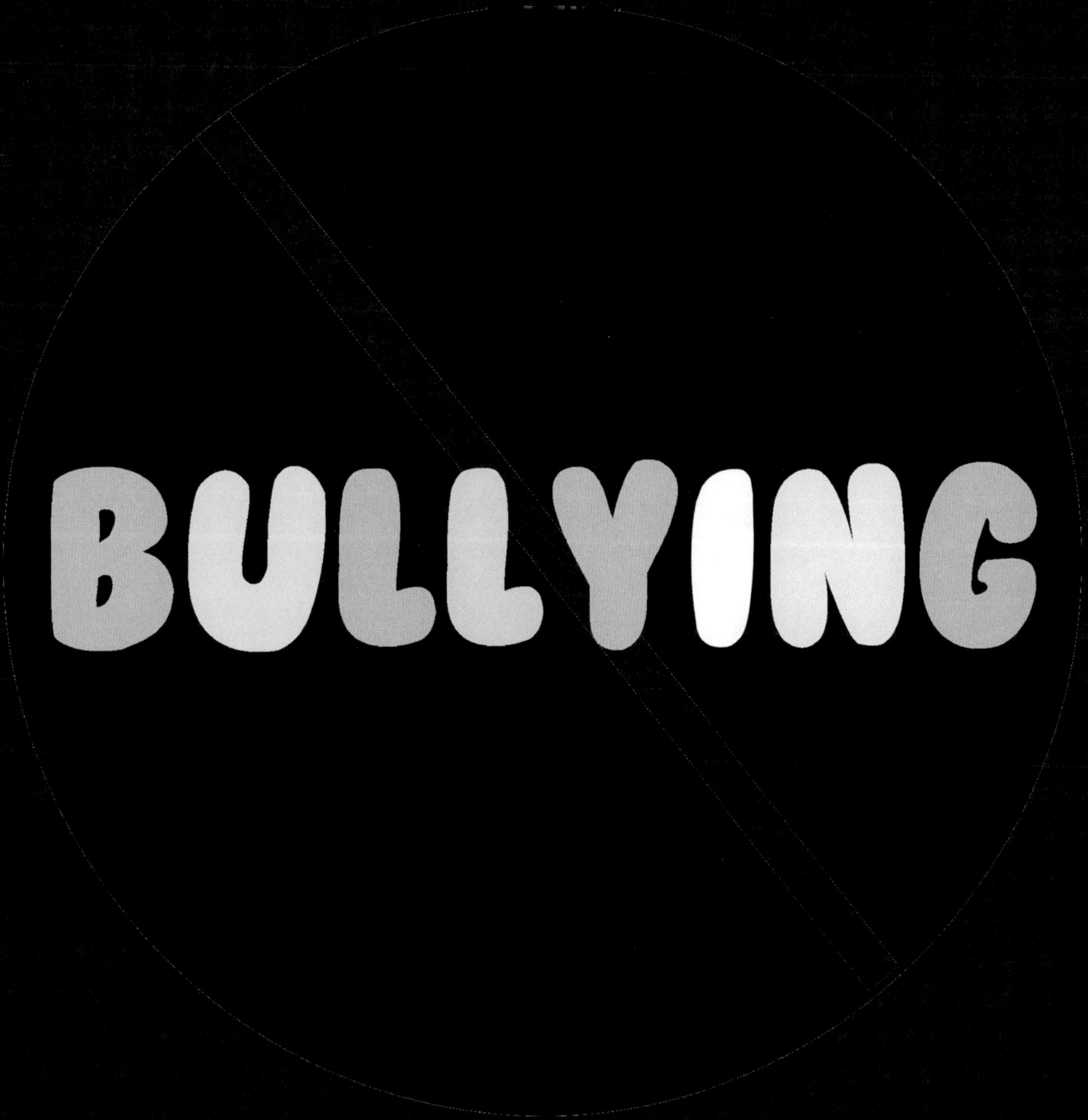
BULLYING

THANKS AGAIN FOR READING MY BOOK. IF YOU LIKED IT, HERE ARE A FEW TITLES YOU MAY BE INTERESTED IN...

# BOOK OF POEMS

I'm like a chicken cluckin'
I'm picking and I'm pluckin'
A plucking and a pickin'
A picking my fat nose

I see the ducks a duckin'
When hunters come a huntin'
They waddle waddle waddle
They waddle as they go

It seems the ducks have fun
Flying high up with the crows
I will stay here on the ground
Mud squishing through my toes

For now I'll keep a cluckin'
A picking and a pluckin'
A plucking and a pickin'
A picking my fat nose

I ASKED THE ANIMALS

# Brenda's Bubble

# Written by Eric C. Corsten
## Illustrated by Megan Toenyes

# GOOOSE

Made in the USA
Columbia, SC
25 August 2021